T0419594

Learn About

WILD WEATHER

HEAT WAVES

by Cody Crane

Children's Press®
An imprint of Scholastic Inc.

Scientific Consultant
Adam Sobel
Columbia University
New York, New York

Reading Consultant
Maggie Peterson
Julia A. Stark Elementary School
Stamford, Connecticut

Library of Congress Cataloging-in-Publication Data available

ISBN 978-1-5461-3599-9 (library binding) / ISBN 978-1-5461-3600-2 (paperback)

10 9 8 7 6 5 4 3 2 1   25 26 27 28 29

Printed in China 62
First edition, 2025

Series produced by Spooky Cheetah Press
Book design by Kathleen Petelinsek

TABLE OF CONTENTS

Introduction

It is summer. You want to play outside, but it is hotter than usual. You are sweating. The place where you live is having a heat wave. You decide to stay inside, where it is cool.

A thermometer shows us how hot or cold it is outside.

Heat waves can happen anywhere on Earth.

CHAPTER 1
What Is a Heat Wave?

The **temperature** tells us how hot or cold it is. During a heat wave, the temperature is higher than normal. The high temperature lasts for more than two days in a row. It does not rain.

Heat waves can last for weeks or months.

Playing in the water is a great way to cool down.

A **drought** is a long period without rain. Heat waves can make droughts worse. Rivers and lakes can dry up. Plants dry up, too. They can burn more easily. That can lead to wildfires.

Wildfires can burn over large areas of land.

Firefighters spray water on a wildfire.

Heat waves can be dangerous. Usually, sweating cools us down. Water **evaporates** from our bodies. It carries away heat. That might not be enough during a heat wave. A person's body temperature could rise too high. They could suffer heatstroke.

A person with heatstroke has to go to the hospital.

Here are some signs a person might have heatstroke.

headache, dizziness

dry, red skin

fast heartbeat

Squirrels "sploot" to stay cool. They lay on their bellies in a shady spot.

A heat wave can harm animals, too. Most animals do not sweat to cool off. Some pant. Water evaporates from their tongues. Others look for shade. That might not be enough during a heat wave.

Zoos often give animals cool treats, like ice pops, during heat waves.

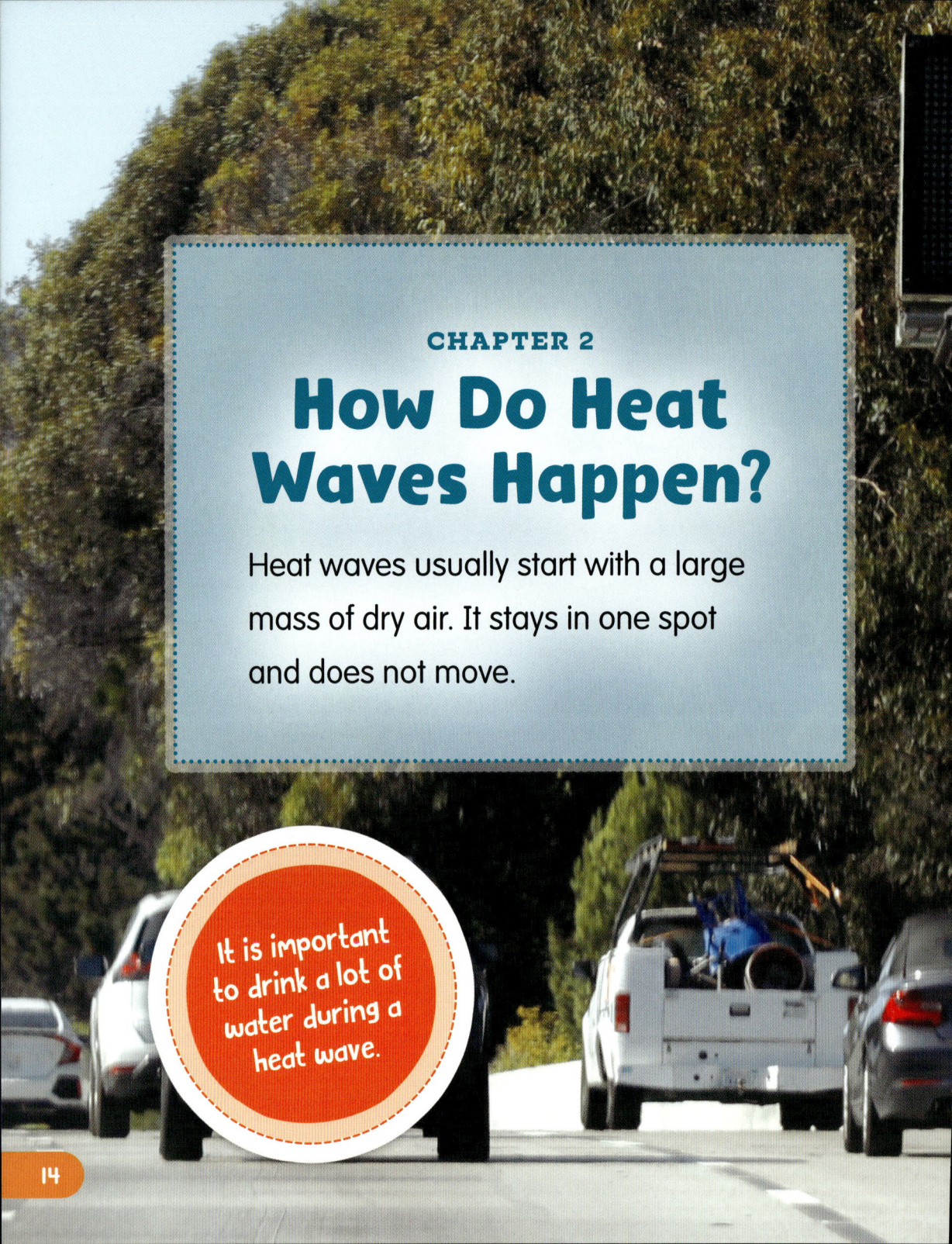

CHAPTER 2

How Do Heat Waves Happen?

Heat waves usually start with a large mass of dry air. It stays in one spot and does not move.

It is important to drink a lot of water during a heat wave.

Cities may warn people about high temperatures.

This is how a heat wave is formed.

1

2

1 The mass of dry air sinks toward the ground. Hot air is trapped underneath.

2 The hot air builds up near the ground.

Hot air acts like a lid on a pot.

3

3

The sky is clear, there are no clouds. That keeps the rain away.

Trees provide shade. They help lower temperatures.

Heat waves are worse in cities than in the countryside. Cities have lots of buildings and roads. Those hold on to heat. Planting trees and other plants can help.

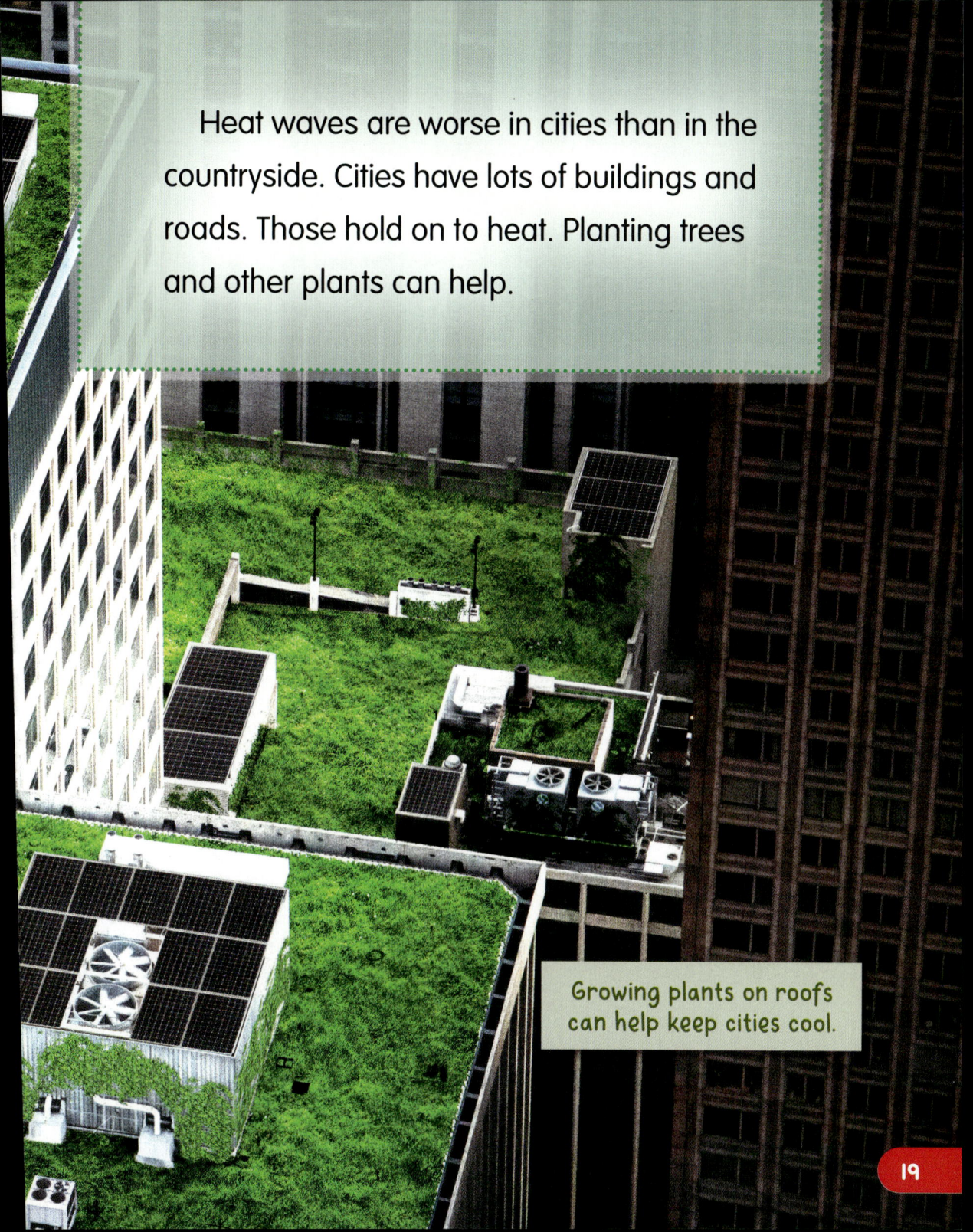

Growing plants on roofs can help keep cities cool.

CHAPTER 3
Predicting Heat Waves

Meteorologists are scientists who **predict** weather. They use tools to see if a heat wave is coming. They also use tools to study heat waves. Take a look at some of those tools here!

A weather **satellite** sails through space. It collects information about the weather.

A thermometer measures air temperature.

A barometer (buh-RAH-mi-tur) measures changes in **air pressure**.

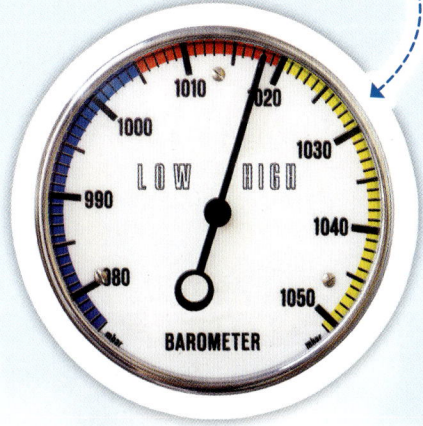

A hygrometer (hye-GRAH-mi-tur) measures temperature and **humidity**. Humidity is the amount of moisture in the air.

A rain gauge collects rain. It shows how much rain has fallen.

Meteorologists give reports about hot weather. The reports often include the heat index. The heat index tells us how hot it feels. The index adds in humidity. When it is humid, it is harder to cool off. That makes it feel even hotter.

The heat index is higher than the actual temperature.

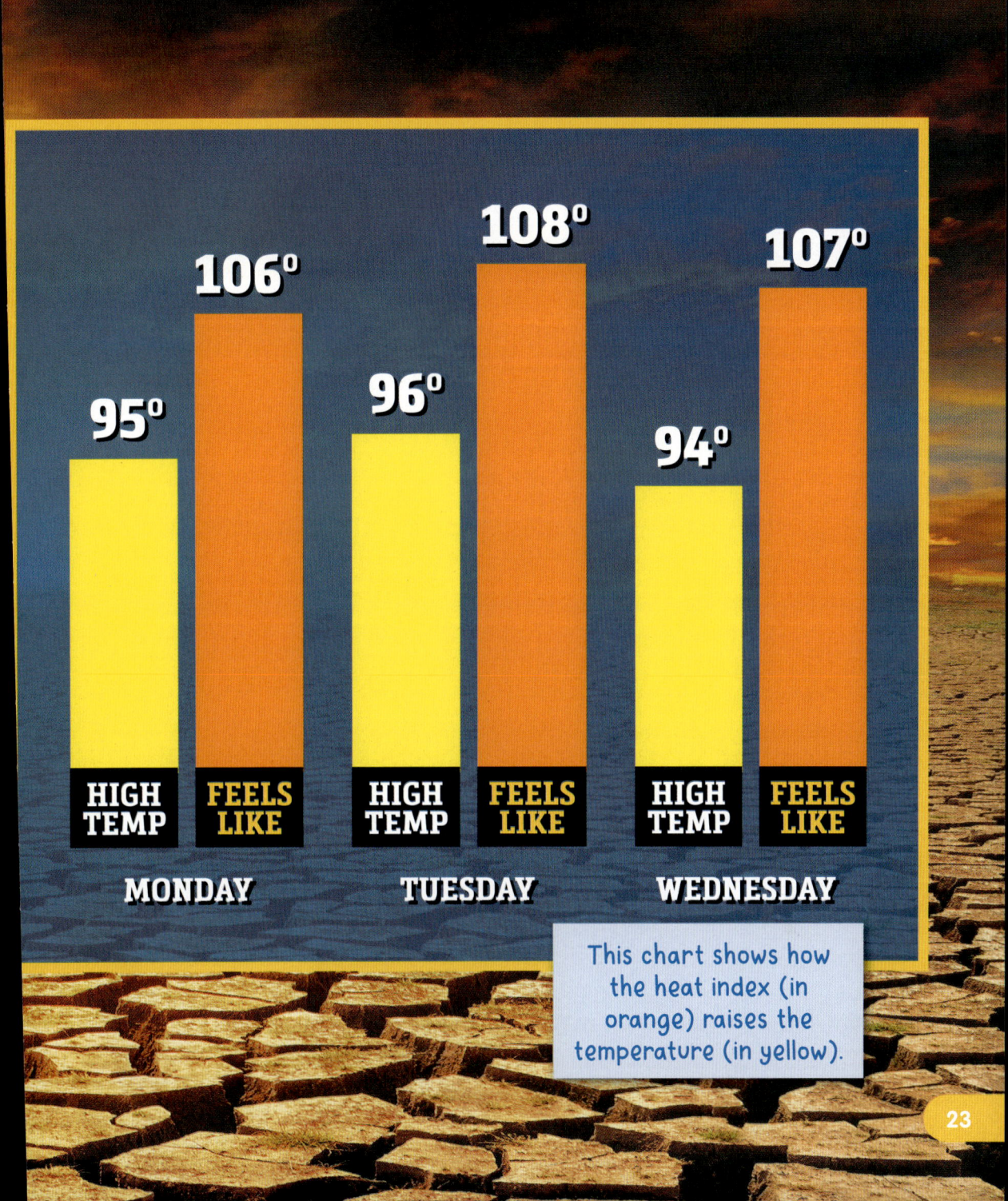

This chart shows how the heat index (in orange) raises the temperature (in yellow).

A heat wave dried up the lake. The boats don't have water to float on.

24

Heat waves are happening more often. They are hotter than they were in the past. And they are lasting longer. Meteorologists think this is happening because of **climate change**. It is causing temperatures around the world to rise.

Some countries in Europe have started naming heat waves. Zoe was a 2022 heat wave.

After some time, a new mass of air will push the dry air mass away. Then the heat wave will end. Until that happens, you can play in the sprinkler or go for a swim. You can visit an air-conditioned library. Just make sure you stay out of the heat!

IF A HEAT WAVE HAPPENS

A heat wave can happen anywhere. The best way to stay safe is to be prepared. Talk to the grown-ups in your house about these steps for staying safe.

Drink Up
You sweat a lot when it is hot. Drink plenty of water to replace those fluids.

Limit Time Outdoors
Play outside only during the coolest parts of the day. That is in the early morning and in the late evening.

Cool Off
Spend time in an air-conditioned building or visit a public pool.

Dress Right
Wear lightweight, loose clothes and a hat to stay cool.

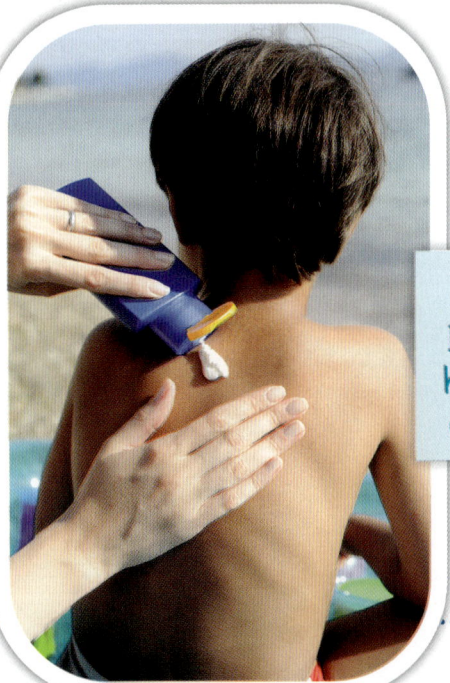

Be Sun Safe
It is easy to get sunburned on hot, clear days. Wear sunblock or a sun shirt when outdoors.

(Turn the page.)

Avoid Hot Cars
The insides of parked cars get very hot. You should never stay inside a parked car when it is hot out.

Help Others
Check on friends and neighbors. Make sure they are staying safe.

Know the Signs
Call 9-1-1 if anyone shows signs of heatstroke (see pages 10–11).

GLOSSARY

air pressure (AIR PRESH-ur) the weight of the air, which is greater near the earth than it is high up

climate change (KLYE-mit CHAYNJ) global warming and other changes in the weather and weather patterns that are happening because of human activity

drought (DROUT) a long period without rain

evaporates (i-VAP-uh-rates) when a liquid, like sweat or water, changes into a vapor or gas

humidity (hyoo-MID-i-tee) the amount of moisture in the air

meteorologists (mee-tee-uh-RAH-luh-jists) experts who study weather

predict (pri-DIKT) to say what will happen in the future

satellite (SAT-uh-lite) a spacecraft that is sent into orbit around the earth, the moon, or another celestial body

temperature (TEM-pur-uh-chur) the degree of heat or cold in something, usually measured by a thermometer

INDEX

ABOUT THE AUTHOR

Cody Crane has written dozens of children's books. She lives with her family in Texas, where heat waves often happen. When they do, she likes to head to the beach!